USBORNE SKILLS

FRACTIONS & DECIMALS

Karen Bryant-Mo

Illustrated by Graham Round

Edited by Kathy Gemmell
Series editor: Jenny Tyler

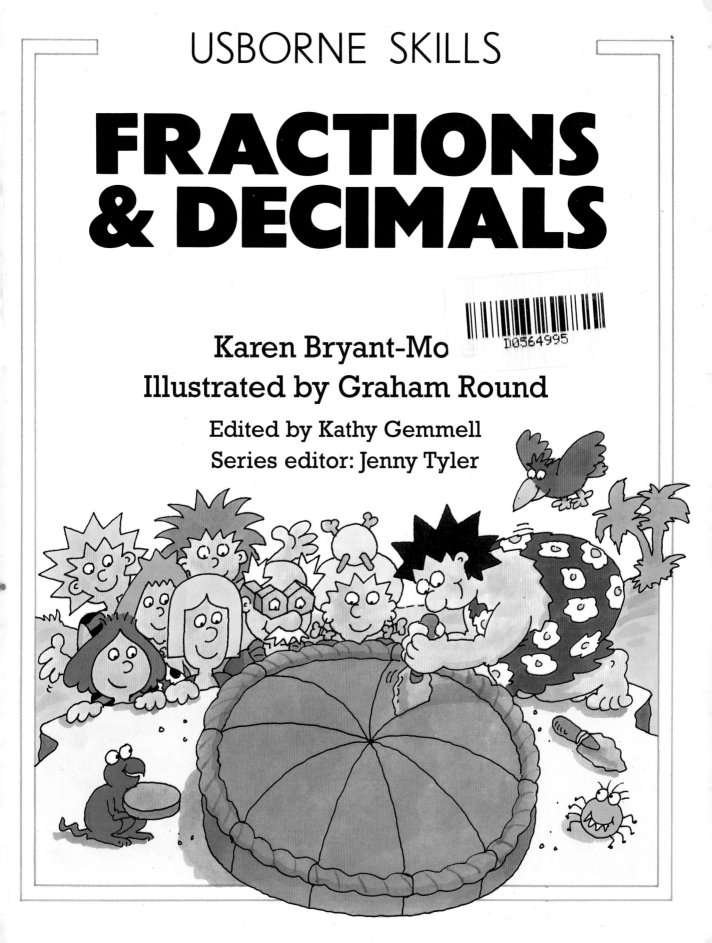

What are fractions?

In this book, you will meet a family called the Ogs. They are going to help you find out about fractions. The Ogs use fractions every day, sometimes without even knowing.

Zog and Mog Og are both hungry, but there is only one rock block left. Mrs. Og tells them to share it. Zog lets Mog cut the block into two pieces, as long as he can choose his piece first.

Mog makes sure that both pieces are exactly the same size.

How can Zog say how much cake he has? His piece isn't 1 whole cake, but nor is it no cake at all. So it must be an amount between zero (0) and one (1).

Numbers that are greater than 0 but smaller than 1 are called **fractions**.

Each piece that Mog has cut is half of 1 cake. A **half**, or one half, is written like this:

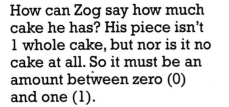

$$\frac{1}{2}$$

The number below the line says how many pieces something has been divided into. The number above the line shows how many of those pieces you are talking about.

This is **1** of those pieces.

The cake has been divided into **2** pieces.

Grandma Og has cut this swampburger into two halves. Both pieces are the same size.

Grandpa Og has cut this swampburger without putting on his glasses. The two pieces are not halves because one piece is bigger than the other.

Things can only be called halves if both pieces are exactly the same size.

With all fractions, the number below the line says how many *equal* pieces something has been divided into.

Grandpa has been decorating arrowheads. He has painted each one with two different paints. Write $\frac{1}{2}$ next to the arrowheads that show halves.

More about the Ogs

Grandma Og

Grandma Og enjoys riding dinosaurs. She has been riding them since she was a girl.

Grandpa Og

Grandpa Og is always happy when he has a paintbrush in his hand.

Mrs. Og

Mrs. Og is a very good singer. She often enters singing competitions.

Mr. Og

Mr. Og is extremely proud of his garden. He spends hours working in it.

Mog Og

Mog Og enjoys gymnastics. She spends a lot of time upside-down.

Zog Og

Zog Og likes getting up early to help out at the Ogtown Dairy.

The Ogs are having a baking session. They have all made huge mud chip cookies. Each cookie is too big for one person to eat, so Grandma Og has decided to cut them all up so they can share them.

Draw a line on each cookie to show where Grandma Og should cut it so that it will be divided into two equal halves.

The slice of pie shop

This is Strudella Struggle's pie shop. Strudella has cut all her pies into slices.

She has put a label into one slice of each pie. Can you help her to work out what fraction of the whole pie that slice is and write it on the label?

Strudella has already labelled the Doubledecker Midge Pie.

I prefer the pie that is in sixths.

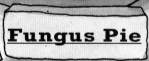

My best pie is cut into thirds.

Remember! The number below the line shows the total number of equal slices in the whole pie. The top number shows the number of slices you are looking at.

$\frac{1}{5}$

Doubledecker Midge Pie

Brontosaurus Pie

Fungus Pie

Bumbleberry Pie

The bottom number is called the **denominator**.

The top number is called the **numerator**.

Chunky Nettle Pie

The Ogs think that all Strudella's pies are delicious, but they each have one pie that they prefer to the rest.

Can you see which pie each person likes best and fill in the table below?

Thirds means 3 equal parts. **Quarters** means 4 equal parts. **Fifths** means 5 equal parts, and so on.

Mr. Og prefers

Grandpa Og prefers

Mrs. Og prefers

Grandma Og prefers

Mog Og prefers

Zog Og prefers

Mammoth Pie

The Ogtown fair

The Ogs live in a town called Ogtown. Every year, Ogtown has a fair. The Ogs are helping to get everything ready for the big day.

Mog Og is holding a blue and orange parasol. Can you spot her? Mog's parasol has eight equal parts and four of those parts are orange. So, $\frac{4}{8}$ of the parasol are orange.

What fraction of the parasol is blue?

The canopy on Mr. Og's Bottle Stall is painted in stripes. $\frac{2}{7}$ are red.

How much is purple?

How much is green?

Grandma's quillboard

The quillboard is made up of four different types of tree bark.

How much is orange Ork bark? [ ]

How much is purple Pooka bark? [ ]

How much is yellow Yog bark? [ ]

How much is green Glug bark? [ ]

Grandpa Og has made decorations and has hung them above the fairground. He knows which paints he wants to use and how much of each paint he will use in each decoration.

Can you use his guide below to fill in the decorations for him?

Sometimes there is more than one correct way to fill in each decoration.

Grandpa's painting guide (from right to left)

First decoration	Second decoration	Third decoration	Fourth decoration	Fifth decoration	Sixth decoration
$\frac{1}{2}$ yellow	$\frac{2}{4}$ orange	$\frac{1}{2}$ pink	$\frac{1}{4}$ yellow	$\frac{1}{4}$ purple	$\frac{2}{4}$ orange
$\frac{1}{2}$ green	$\frac{1}{4}$ blue	$\frac{1}{2}$ purple	$\frac{2}{4}$ orange	$\frac{1}{4}$ blue	$\frac{2}{4}$ green
	$\frac{1}{4}$ red		$\frac{1}{4}$ blue	$\frac{1}{4}$ red	
				$\frac{1}{4}$ green	

Seventh decoration	Eighth decoration	Ninth decoration	Tenth decoration	Eleventh decoration	Twelfth decoration
$\frac{1}{3}$ yellow	$\frac{1}{2}$ green	$\frac{2}{4}$ blue	$\frac{1}{3}$ orange	$\frac{3}{8}$ yellow	$\frac{1}{4}$ red
$\frac{2}{3}$ purple	$\frac{1}{2}$ red	$\frac{2}{4}$ pink	$\frac{1}{3}$ yellow	$\frac{3}{8}$ blue	$\frac{1}{4}$ green
			$\frac{1}{3}$ green	$\frac{2}{8}$ pink	$\frac{2}{4}$ orange

9

The Ogs' garden

Grandpa Og and Mr. and Mrs. Og are all busy in the garden.

Mr. Og has just finished building the garden wall. He used lots of bricks of different sizes. However, all the bricks in the same row are the same size. Zog has realized that he can use the wall to help him understand fractions.

How?

$\frac{1}{3}$ $\frac{1}{3}$ $\frac{1}{3}$

$\frac{1}{2}$ $\frac{1}{2}$

Each of the bricks on the bottom row is half the length of the whole wall, so Zog writes $\frac{1}{2}$ on each brick.

Each of the bricks on the next row up is one third of the length of the whole wall, so he writes $\frac{1}{3}$ on each brick.

Can you finish writing the fractions on the wall for Zog?

Grandpa's flowers

Grandpa Og has been growing exotic flowers. $\frac{4}{8}$ of the petals on the flower he is smelling are red.

10

Count along 4 bricks on the top row of Mr. Og's wall. That is $\frac{4}{8}$. Now draw a straight line down to the bottom row with your finger. You will see that $\frac{4}{8}$ is the same as $\frac{1}{2}$.

Can you help Grandpa Og find two different ways of describing the fraction of red petals on the other flowers? Use the wall to help you. Write the answers on the flowerpots.

I have written $\frac{4}{8}$ or $\frac{1}{2}$ on this flowerpot.

$\frac{4}{8}$ or $\frac{1}{2}$

Different fractions that mean the same amount are called **equivalent fractions**.

Use Mr. Og's wall to help Mrs. Og decide how many apples to pick from each of these trees.

She wants to pick $\frac{2}{3}$ of the apples on tree 1, $\frac{1}{2}$ of the apples on tree 2 and $\frac{3}{4}$ of the apples on tree 3.

Use crayons to fill in the number of apples she will pick from each tree.

Reptile Road

The Ogs live in Reptile Road. As part of the Ogtown festival, the Ogs and their friends are entering Reptile Road in the Best Kept Street competition.

Today, everyone is cleaning windows. Each of the windows in the Ogs' house has 4 panes. Mog has cleaned 7 panes. That can be called $\frac{7}{4}$ because each window has 4 panes the same size and she has cleaned 7 of them.

It can also be called $1\frac{3}{4}$ because she has cleaned 1 whole window and 3 out of 4 equal sized panes.

I've cleaned $\frac{7}{4}$ or $1\frac{3}{4}$

P.P.C.

P.P.C.

I've cleaned

or

A cross-bog run

Mrs. Og is planning a cross-bog run for the family. She has drawn a map of the route.

Distances in Ogtown are measured in megastrides. The cross-bog route is 40 megastrides long. Mrs. Og has marked the megastrides on the map.

To make sure that everyone takes the right paths, Mrs. Og is going to draw some signs to show what they should be passing.

Three-quarters of the way around the course they should pass a windmill, so Mrs. Og has drawn a windmill sign at the point that is $\frac{3}{4}$ of 40 megastrides.

To work out fractions of a number, you need to divide that number by the bottom number of the fraction then multiply your answer by the top number.

This is how you work out $\frac{3}{4}$ of 40:

40 divided by 4 is 10.
10 multiplied by 3 is 30.
So, $\frac{3}{4}$ of 40 is 30.

If you are not sure how to divide and multiply, there is another way to do this.

Find a pack of cards and count out 40. Put the rest back. Whatever fraction you have to find, you deal the cards into the same number of piles as the bottom number. Then you count up the cards in the same number of piles as the top number.

So, with $\frac{3}{4}$, you would deal the cards into 4 equal piles and count the total number of cards in 3 of those piles.

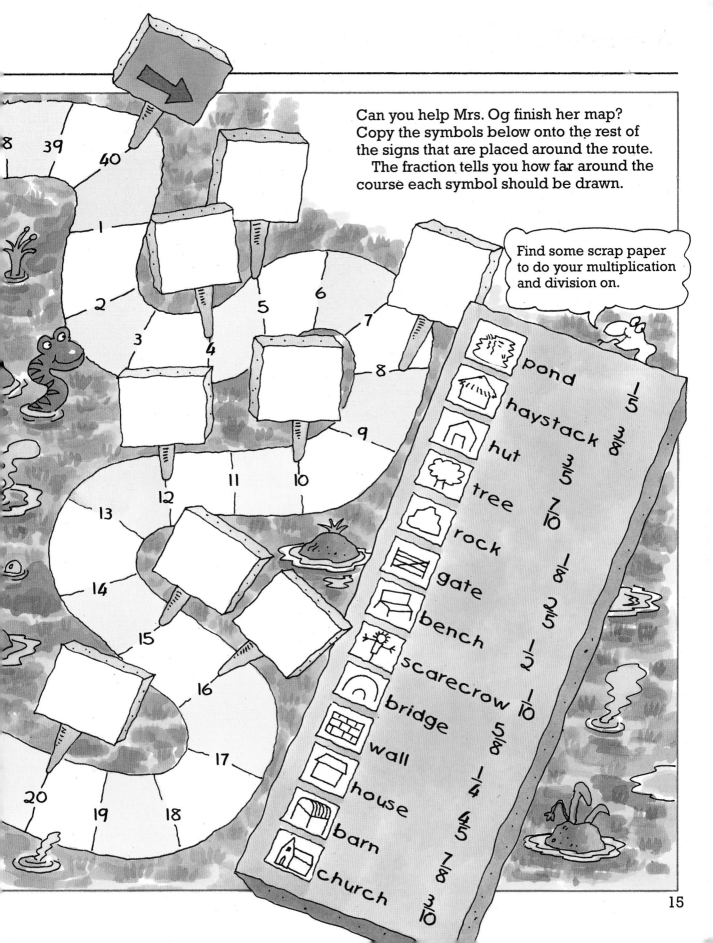

Can you help Mrs. Og finish her map?
Copy the symbols below onto the rest of
the signs that are placed around the route.
The fraction tells you how far around the
course each symbol should be drawn.

Find some scrap paper
to do your multiplication
and division on.

pond $\frac{1}{5}$

haystack $\frac{3}{8}$

hut $\frac{3}{5}$

tree $\frac{7}{10}$

rock $\frac{1}{8}$

gate $\frac{2}{5}$

bench $\frac{1}{2}$

scarecrow $\frac{1}{10}$

bridge $\frac{5}{8}$

wall $\frac{1}{4}$

house $\frac{4}{5}$

barn $\frac{7}{8}$

church $\frac{3}{10}$

The dairy

Zog has a Saturday job at the Ogtown Dairy. He gets up very early to help put the milk into crates. He then sorts out the crates so that they are ready for delivery.

There is 1 bottle in the crate next to Zog. Each crate can hold 10 bottles. So, 1 bottle takes up $\frac{1}{10}$ of a crate.

There is another way to think of $\frac{1}{10}$ and that is to call it 0.1.

The 0 shows that there are no full crates. The dot is called a **decimal point**. The number that comes after the decimal point shows the number of tenths.

Decimals are just another way of writing fractions which are tenths or hundredths.

There is a sticker on the front of each crate. It tells Zog how full the crates should be.

Can you draw in the correct number of bottle tops and then write the fraction as a decimal on the other sticker?

Mammoth Milk

All the crates are full apart from the top ones.

Zog's next job is to load up some crates that have already been stacked. Use the delivery slab on the right to work out which stack is going to which road, then write the name of the road on the label.

Delivery slab

Swamp Street	1.5 crates
Allosaurus Avenue	3.8 crates
Brontosaurus Boulevard	2.4 crates
Reptile Road	3.2 crates
Dinosaur Drive	1.8 crates

Radio Ogtown

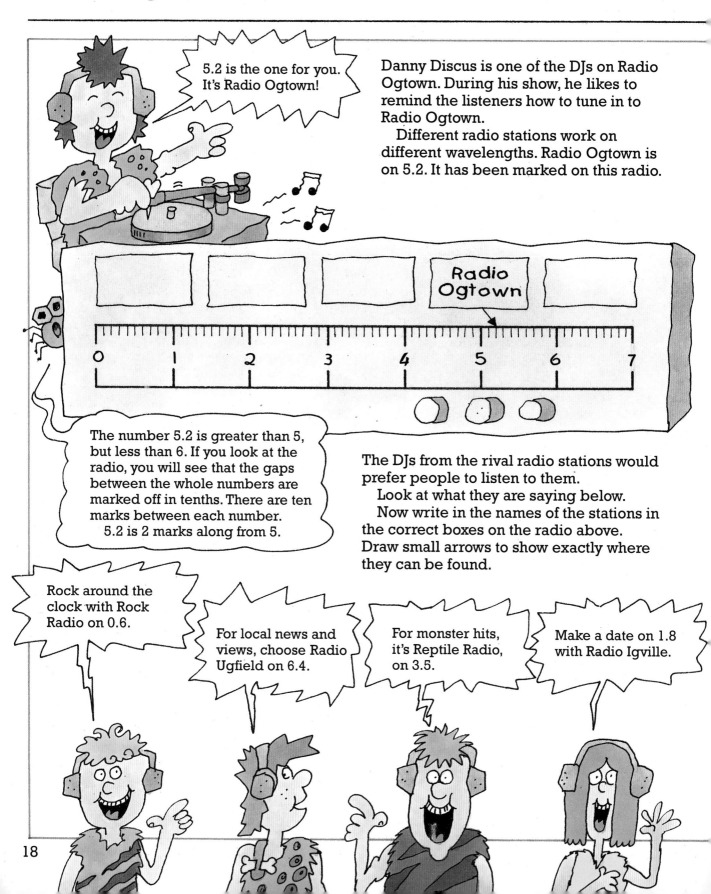

5.2 is the one for you. It's Radio Ogtown!

Danny Discus is one of the DJs on Radio Ogtown. During his show, he likes to remind the listeners how to tune in to Radio Ogtown.

Different radio stations work on different wavelengths. Radio Ogtown is on 5.2. It has been marked on this radio.

The number 5.2 is greater than 5, but less than 6. If you look at the radio, you will see that the gaps between the whole numbers are marked off in tenths. There are ten marks between each number.
5.2 is 2 marks along from 5.

The DJs from the rival radio stations would prefer people to listen to them.
Look at what they are saying below.
Now write in the names of the stations in the correct boxes on the radio above. Draw small arrows to show exactly where they can be found.

Rock around the clock with Rock Radio on 0.6.

For local news and views, choose Radio Ugfield on 6.4.

For monster hits, it's Reptile Radio, on 3.5.

Make a date on 1.8 with Radio Igville.

18

Every Wednesday evening, Danny Discus holds a talent contest live on the radio.

Mrs. Og has entered this week and all the rest of the Og family have come along to cheer her on.

The contestants get points according to how hard the audience claps.

The clapping is measured on a clapometer. The louder the clapping, the higher up the clapometer the red line moves.

Clapometer results

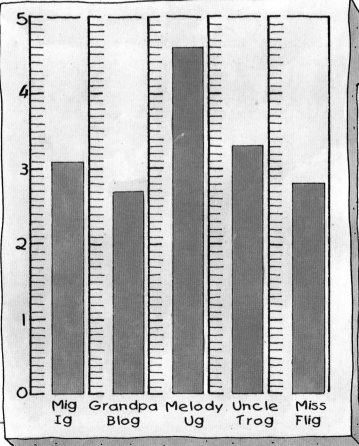

Mrs. Og has scored 3.9. On the left are the other contestants' results. Can you write their scores on the scoreboard below and then write down their position in the competition?

Contestant	Score	Position
Mrs. Og	3.9	
Mig Ig		
Grandpa Blog		
Melody Ug		
Uncle Trog		
Miss Flig		

The gymnastics competition

Mog and Zog Og and Mig and Tig Ig have entered a gymnastics competition. The judges are watching them perform.

The maximum score for each exercise is 10. Every time the contestants make a mistake, they lose points. Read the paragraphs beside each picture. They tell you how many points Mog, Zog, Mig and Tig have lost. Add up the total number of points lost by each person, using the judges' noterocks below. Mog's has been done for you.

Mog has just finished her branch routine. She lost 0.1 points for stopping between swings and 0.5 points for jumping back with two feet when she landed.

Adding decimals is easy. It is just the same as ordinary adding, but you must remember to write all the decimal points under each other.

Mig is vaulting the brontobox. She loses 0.1 points for having one leg bent and 0.3 points for moving one foot when she landed.

Mog

$$0.1$$
$$+ 0.5$$
$$\overline{0.6}$$

Zog

Tig is on the slab. He falls off once and loses 0.5 points. He also wobbles and puts his hands down which loses him another 0.5 points. One of his jumps is not high enough. This costs him 0.2 points.

Zog is in the middle of his mud routine. He loses 0.1 points for an unpointed toe and 0.2 points because he does not hold his handstand for long enough.

Scoreboard

Mog

Zog

Tig

Mig

Now take each person's total away from 10 and write the answer on the scoreboard above.

You will probably find it easiest to write 10.0 and then write the number of points lost underneath.

Mog would work out her score like this:

$$\begin{array}{r} 10.0 \\ -\ 0.6 \end{array}$$

Work out the answer in the usual way, but remember the decimal point.

The bucking bronto

The Ogs have come to Rodeo Ranch to ride the wild dinosaurs. The idea is to see how long they can sit on the back of a dinosaur before it throws them off.

The dinosaurs all think it is great fun. They enjoy trying to throw their riders. They are so strong that the riders never last longer than a few seconds.

Strug times the riders with his stopwatch. He could time the riders in tenths of a second, but that would not be precise enough. Instead, he times them in hundredths of a second.

I stayed on for twenty-two seconds and eight hundredths of a second.

I stayed on for seven seconds and four hundredths of a second.

To use hundredths of a second, you need to write two numbers after the decimal point. So, 3 seconds and 24 hundredths of a second would be written as 3.24 seconds.

22

I only stayed on for three seconds and seventy-one hundredths of a second.

I stayed on for twelve seconds and thirty-two hundredths of a second.

I stayed on for fourteen seconds and sixty-three hundredths of a second.

I stayed on for eighteen seconds and fifty-nine hundredths of a second.

Read what the Ogs are saying. Strug has filled in Mrs. Og's time on the chart. Can you fill in the others for him? Use whole numbers, a decimal point and two numbers after the decimal point.

Watch out! One second and one hundredth of a second is written 1.01 not 1.1. 1.1 is one second and ten hundredths (or one tenth) of a second.

Write 1st next to the time of the person who stayed on the longest, 2nd next to the time of the person who stayed on the second longest and so on.

Who was the winner?

Name	Time in seconds	Place
Mrs. Og	7.04	
Mr. Og		
Grandma Og		
Grandpa Og		
Mog		
Zog		

Mr. Trog's deliveries

The Ogs' friend, Mr. Trog, owns a general store in Ogtown.

As part of the service he offers his customers, he will deliver orders to the villages around Ogtown.

This map shows Ogtown and the area around it. The Ogtown measurement, megastrides, is usually shortened to ms. There are 100 strides in a megastride. So one stride is one hundredth of a megastride, or 0.01ms.

Mr. Trog likes to keep a note of the distances he travels in his van. He writes everything in his diary.

Mr. Trog's diary

Mon	Ogtown to Ugling to Little Fern to Ogtown
Tues	Ogtown to Old Rock (through Ugling) and back
Wed	Ogtown to Fossiltown to Ugling to Little Fern to Ogtown
Thurs	Ogtown to Fossiltown and back
Fri	Ogtown to Fossiltown to Swampville to Little Fern to Ogtown
Sat	Ogtown to Ugling to Old Rock to Fossiltown to Ogtown

Little Fern
Old Rock
Ugling

2.47ms

Igville

Fossiltown
7.63ms
Old Rock

Can you help Mr. Trog add up the distances he travels each day and write them on his noterock below?

Mon

Tues

Wed

Thurs

Fri

Sat

Can you work out how many more megastrides he drove on Tuesday than on Thursday?

How many more megastrides did he drive on Wednesday than on Saturday?

Adding and subtracting with two decimal places is just as easy as doing it with one decimal place. Don't forget the decimal point.

The coconut game

Mog and Zog are both standing at the bottom of palm trees. They both want to climb their trees and get the coconut.

You can play a game to see who gets to the coconut first. You will need two counters or coins and a dice.

You can play by yourself or with a friend. To play with two players, you each choose who you would like to be and put a coin or counter on the word "Start" at the bottom of your tree.

Each player rolls the dice three times. Write down the numbers as you throw them, except for the 1's. When you roll a 1, write it down as a decimal point.

So [⚄] then [⚀] then [⚂] is 5.3

Or [⚀] then [⚄] then [⚂] is .53

If you get more than one decimal point, you roll again until you get another number on the dice.

> It doesn't matter where the decimal point comes, or if you don't roll one at all.

The players then compare their numbers and the person with the greater number moves up one space on the tree.

The winner is the first person to jump from the last space onto the coconut.

Start

A good way to start working out whether one number is greater than another number is to look at the whole numbers. 5.6 is greater than .72 because there are 5 whole numbers in 5.6 and none in .72.

If you end up with a number like 43., that is just the same as 43 whole numbers.

If both players roll a decimal point followed by two numbers, you can compare them just as easily as whole numbers. .76 is greater than .58 because 76 hundredths are greater than 58 hundredths.

If you want to play the game by yourself, you can roll the dice for both Zog and Mog and see who wins.

Start

Answers

Page 3

Page 5

Pages 6 and 7

Pages 8 and 9

The Ogtown fair

The Ogs live in a town called Ogtown. Every year, Ogtown has a fair. The Ogs are helping to get everything ready for the big day.

Mog Og is holding a blue and orange parasol. Can you spot her? Mog's parasol has eight equal parts and four of those parts are orange. So, $\frac{4}{8}$ of the parasol are orange.

What fraction of the parasol is blue? [$\frac{4}{8}$]

Grandma's quillboard

The quillboard is made up of four different types of tree bark.

How much is orange Ork bark? [$\frac{3}{20}$]
How much is purple Pooka bark? [$\frac{6}{20}$]
How much is yellow Yog bark? [$\frac{4}{20}$]
How much is green Glug bark? [$\frac{7}{20}$]

The canopy on Mr. Og's Bottle Stall is painted in stripes. $\frac{3}{7}$ are red.

How much is purple? [$\frac{3}{7}$]
How much is green? [$\frac{2}{7}$]

Grandpa Og has made decorations and has hung them above the fairground. He knows which paints he wants to use and how much of each paint he will use in each decoration.
Can you use his guide below to fill in the decorations for him?

Sometimes there is more than one correct way to fill in each decoration.

You can fill in the decorations in several ways. Check that the number of parts you have filled in with any one crayon or felt tip pen is the same as the top number in the fraction written on the guide.

Grandpa's painting guide (from right to left)

First decoration	Second decoration	Third decoration	Fourth decoration	Fifth decoration	Sixth decoration
yellow	orange	pink	yellow	purple	orange
green	blue	purple	orange	blue	green
	red		blue	red	

Seventh decoration	Eighth decoration	Ninth decoration	Tenth decoration	Eleventh decoration	Twelfth decoration
yellow	green	blue	orange	yellow	red
purple	red	pink	yellow	blue	green
			green	pink	orange

8

Pages 10 and 11

The Ogs' garden

Grandpa Og and Mr. and Mrs. Og are all busy in the garden.

Mr. Og has just finished building the garden wall. He used lots of bricks of different sizes. However, all the bricks in the same row are the same size. Zog has realized that he can use the wall to help him understand fractions.

How?

$\frac{1}{8}$	$\frac{1}{8}$	$\frac{1}{8}$	$\frac{1}{8}$	$\frac{1}{8}$	$\frac{1}{8}$
$\frac{1}{6}$	$\frac{1}{6}$	$\frac{1}{6}$	$\frac{1}{6}$	$\frac{1}{6}$	$\frac{1}{6}$
$\frac{1}{4}$		$\frac{1}{4}$		$\frac{1}{4}$	$\frac{1}{4}$
$\frac{1}{3}$		$\frac{1}{3}$		$\frac{1}{3}$	
$\frac{1}{2}$			$\frac{1}{2}$		$\frac{1}{2}$

Each of the bricks on the bottom row is half the length of the whole wall, so Zog writes $\frac{1}{2}$ on each brick.
Each of the bricks on the next row up is one third of the length of the whole wall, so he writes $\frac{1}{3}$ on each brick.
Can you finish writing the fractions on the wall for Zog?

Grandpa's flowers

Grandpa Og has been growing exotic flowers. $\frac{1}{6}$ of the petals on the flower he is smelling are red.

Count along 4 bricks on the top row of Mr. Og's wall. That is $\frac{4}{8}$. Now draw a straight line down to the bottom row with your finger. You will see that $\frac{4}{8}$ is the same as $\frac{1}{2}$.
Can you help Grandpa Og find two different ways of describing the fraction of red petals on the other flowers? Use the wall to help you. Write the answers on the flowerpots.

I have written $\frac{1}{2}$ or on this flowerpot.

$\frac{6}{8}$ or $\frac{3}{4}$ $\frac{2}{6}$ or $\frac{1}{3}$ $\frac{2}{8}$ or $\frac{1}{4}$ $\frac{4}{6}$ or $\frac{2}{3}$

Different fractions that mean the same amount are called **equivalent fractions**.

Use Mr. Og's wall to help Mrs. Og decide how many apples to pick from each of these trees.
She wants to pick $\frac{1}{3}$ of the apples on tree 1, $\frac{1}{2}$ of the apples on tree 2 and $\frac{1}{4}$ of the apples on tree 3.
Use crayons to fill in the number of apples she will pick from each tree.

10

11

29

Pages 12 and 13

Reptile Road

The Ogs live in Reptile Road. As part of the Ogtown festival, the Ogs and their friends are entering Reptile Road in the Best Kept Street competition.

Today, everyone is cleaning windows. Each of the windows in the Ogs' house has 4 panes. Mog has cleaned 7 panes. That can be called $\frac{7}{4}$ because each window has 4 panes the same size and she has cleaned 7 of them.

It can also be called $1\frac{3}{4}$ because she has cleaned 1 whole window and 3 out of 4 equal sized panes.

Can you finish filling in all the speech bubbles?

The residents of Reptile Road are so busy that they have decided to order pizzas to be delivered for lunch. Each whole pizza is cut into 6 slices and each family orders the number of sixths they want.

Can you work out how many whole pizzas and how many sixths each family will get?

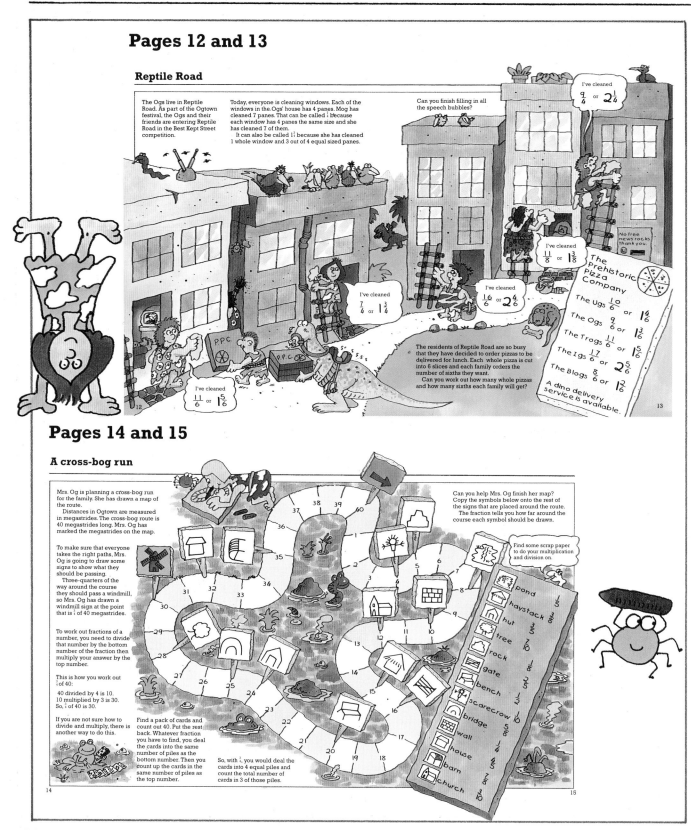

Pages 14 and 15

A cross-bog run

Mrs. Og is planning a cross-bog run for the family. She has drawn a map of the route.

Distances in Ogtown are measured in megastrides. The cross-bog route is 40 megastrides long. Mrs. Og has marked the megastrides on the map.

To make sure that everyone takes the right paths, Mrs. Og is going to draw some signs to show what they should be passing.

Three-quarters of the way around the course they should pass a windmill, so Mrs. Og has drawn a windmill sign at the point that is $\frac{3}{4}$ of 40 megastrides.

To work out fractions of a number, you need to divide that number by the bottom number of the fraction then multiply your answer by the top number.

This is how you work out $\frac{3}{4}$ of 40:

40 divided by 4 is 10.
10 multiplied by 3 is 30.
So, $\frac{3}{4}$ of 40 is 30.

If you are not sure how to divide and multiply, there is another way to do this.

Find a pack of cards and count out 40. Put the rest back. Whatever fraction you have to find, you deal the cards into the same number of piles as the bottom number. Then you count up the cards in the same number of piles as the top number.

So, with $\frac{3}{4}$, you would deal the cards into 4 equal piles and count the total number of cards in 3 of those piles.

Can you help Mrs. Og finish her map? Copy the symbols below onto the rest of the signs that are placed around the route.

The fraction tells you how far around the course each symbol should be drawn.

Find some scrap paper to do your multiplication and division on.

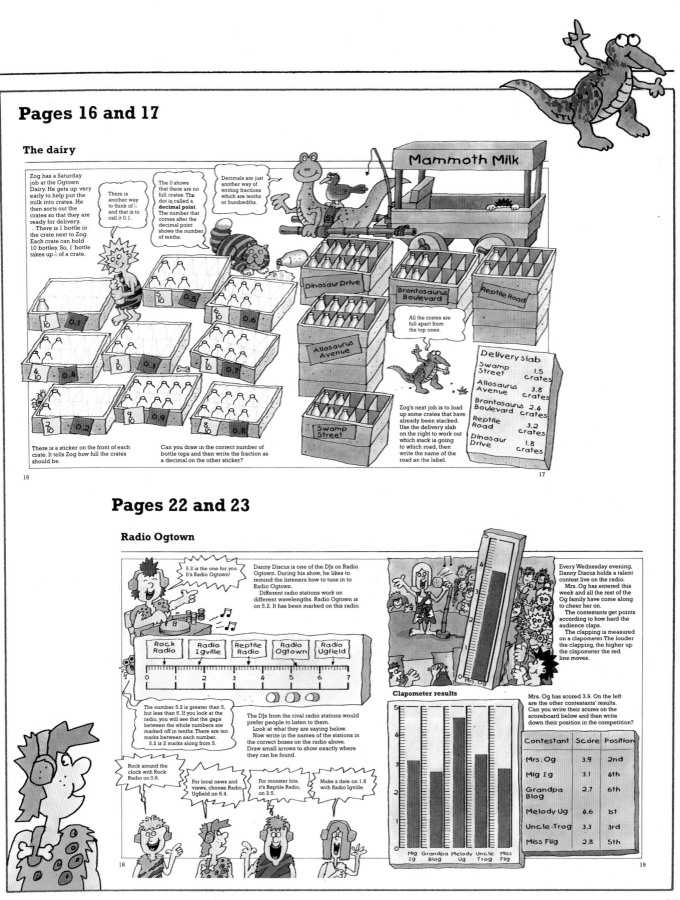

Pages 20 and 21

The gymnastics competition

Mog and Zog Og and Mig and Tig Ig have entered a gymnastics competition. The judges are watching them perform.

The maximum score for each exercise is 10. Every time the contestants make a mistake, they lose points. Read the paragraphs beside each picture. They tell you how many points Mog, Zog, Mig and Tig have lost. Add up the total number of points lost by each person, using the judges' noterocks below. Mog's has been done for you.

Tig is on the slab. He falls off, once and loses 0.5 points. He also wobbles and puts his hands down which loses him another 0.5 points. One of his jumps is not high enough. This costs him 0.2 points.

Zog is in the middle of his mud routine. He loses 0.1 points for an unpointed toe and 0.2 points because he does not hold his handstand for long enough.

Mog has just finished her branch routine. She lost 0.1 points for stopping between swings and 0.5 points for jumping back with two feet when she landed.

Mig is vaulting the brontobox. She loses 0.1 points for having one leg bent and 0.3 points for moving one foot when she landed.

Adding decimals is easy. It is just the same as ordinary adding, but you must remember to write all the decimal points under each other.

Scoreboard

Mog	9.4
Zog	9.7
Tig	8.8
Mig	9.6

Now take each person's total away from 10 and write the answer on the scoreboard above.

You will probably find it easiest to write 10.0 and then write the number of points lost underneath.

Mog would work out her score like this:
```
  10.0
-  0.6
```

Work out the answer in the usual way, but remember the decimal point.

Mog
```
  0.1
+ 0.5
-----
  0.6
```

Zog
```
  0.1
+ 0.2
-----
  0.3
```

Tig
```
  0.5
  0.5
+ 0.2
-----
  1.2
```

Mig
```
  0.1
+ 0.3
-----
  0.4
```

20

21

Page 23

I only stayed on for three seconds and seventy-one hundredths of a second.

I stayed on for twelve seconds and thirty-two hundredths of a second.

I stayed on for fourteen seconds and sixty-three hundredths of a second.

I stayed on for eighteen seconds and fifty-nine hundredths of a second.

Read what the Ogs are saying. Strug has filled in Mrs. Og's time on the chart. Can you fill in the others for him? Use whole numbers, a decimal point and two numbers after the decimal point.

Watch out! One second and one hundredth of a second is written 1.01 not 1.1. 1.1 is one second and ten hundredths (or one tenth) of a second.

Write 1st next to the time of the person who stayed on the longest, 2nd next to the time of the person who stayed on the second longest and so on.

Who was the winner? [Zog]

Name	Time in seconds	Place
Mrs. Og	7.04	
Mr. Og	18.59	5th
Grandma Og	12.32	2nd
Grandpa Og	3.71	6th
Mog	14.63	4th
Zog	22.08	3rd
		1st

23

Page 25

Mr. Trog's diary

Mon	Ogtown to Ugling to Little Fern to Ogtown
Tues	Ogtown to Old Rock (through Ugling) and back
Wed	Ogtown to Fossiltown to Ugling to Little Fern to Ogtown
Thurs	Ogtown to Fossiltown and back
Fri	Ogtown to Fossiltown to Swampville to Little Fern to Ogtown
Sat	Ogtown to Ugling to Old Rock to Fossiltown to Ogtown

Mr. Trog likes to keep a note of the distances he travels in his van. He writes everything in his diary.

Little Fern — Old Rock

Ugling

2.47ms

Igville

1.63ms

Fossiltown — Old Rock

Can you help Mr. Trog add up the distances he travels each day and write them on his noterock below?

Mon	8.17ms
Tues	8.58ms
Wed	14.89ms
Thurs	6.54ms
Fri	12.65ms
Sat	11.75ms

Can you work out how many more megastrides he drove on Tuesday than on Thursday?

[2.04ms]

How many more megastrides did he drive on Wednesday than on Saturday?

[3.16ms]

Adding and subtracting with two decimal places is just as easy as doing it with one decimal place. Don't forget the decimal point.

25
